T0197478

My Favorite Night of the Year

Ceretha Lawson

To order additional copies of this book, contact:
Xlibris
844-714-8691
www.Xlibris.com
Orders@Xlibris.com

ISBN:	Softcover	978-1-6698-2170-0
	Hardcover	978-1-6698-2171-7
	EBook	978-1-6698-2169-4

Print information available on the last page

Rev. date: 04/26/2022

My Favorite Night of the Year

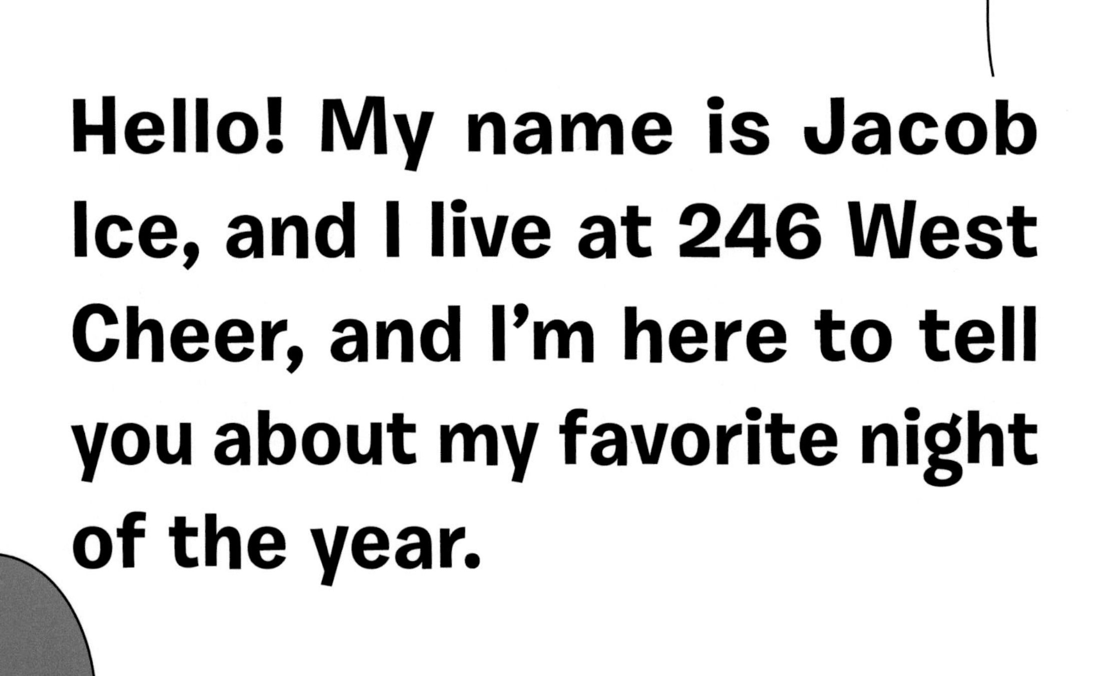

Hello! My name is Jacob Ice, and I live at 246 West Cheer, and I'm here to tell you about my favorite night of the year.

It's not a holiday like Christmas or Halloween or any of the ones that fall in between.

It is August 30, a very special day when all my family come over to celebrate Grandma's birthday.

APPY BIRTHDA
GRANDMA
BIRTHDAY

We have lots of food like Thanksgiving and plenty of candy like Halloween.

We even have hats and whistles like we have on New Year's Eve.

There are fireworks like the Fourth of July and lots of presents like Christmas Day.

She gets lots of cards and crafts just like she does on Mother's Day.

HAPY BIRTHDAY
GRANDMA
HAPPY BIRTHDAY
HAPPY BIRTHDAY
HAPPY BIRTHDAY
HAPPY BIRTHDAY
HAPPY BIRTHDAY
HAPPY BIRTHDAY GRANDMA

There's even a band marching like the back-to-school parade.

Everyone has on their finest garments like Easter Sunday, and Grandma gets all the hugs and kisses like it's her very own Valentine's Day.

IN LOVING MEMORY

OF MY GRANDMTHERS

FANNIE
MAY
WASHINGTON

GLORIA
JEAN
JOHNSON

Printed in the United States
by Baker & Taylor Publisher Services